Jenny the Pony's Big Day

Jenny the Pony's Big Day

Liz Kessler and Laura Tonge

Illustrated by
Mike Phillips

Orion
Children's Books

ORION CHILDREN'S BOOKS

First published in Great Britain in 2017
by Hodder and Stoughton

1 3 5 7 9 10 8 6 4 2

A CIP catalogue record for this book
is available from the British Library.

ISBN 978 1 4440 1596 6

Printed and bound in China

The paper and board used in this book are from well-managed forests
and other responsible sources.

Orion Children's Books
An imprint of
Hachette Children's Group
Part of Hodder and Stoughton
Carmelite House
50 Victoria Embankment
London EC4Y 0DZ

An Hachette UK Company
www.hachette.co.uk

www.orionchildrensbooks.co.uk

*Dedicated to the fabulous Lottie, with
thanks for your help and inspiration*

Contents

Chapter One

It was a sunny Saturday in spring and there was a buzz in the air. Sophie whistled as she brought in the horses. Jade, the head girl, hummed a tune as she swept the yard. Even Marion, the owner of the yard, was smiling.

'What's everyone so excited about?' Jenny wondered.

'The Spring Gala is only a month away,' said Jade, as she and Sophie walked across the yard with Jenny.

'I can't wait,' said Sophie.
'I'm going to enter Showing and
Jumping.'

'Better get practising,' Jade
called as she went off to look for a
wheelbarrow.

'Don't forget to groom Jenny,'
Marion called on her way past.

'Good luck with that,' thought Jenny. She had spent all day in the field rolling around with her friends and had the messiest mane on the yard.

She was so muddy that it hurt to
brush her, and she kept pulling away.

The girls did their best, then they
left Jenny in her stable.

Chapter Two

'Lesson time!' Marion called.
Sam tried to take Jenny to the
mounting block. But Jenny had
her own ideas.

She hadn't seen her friends
Sooty and Hobnob for a while.

Eventually Sam gave in and let her lead him away from the mounting block, and across to the hay bales where Sooty and Hobnob were snuggled up sleeping.

'Come on, let's get to your lesson,' Marion said.

Jenny finally let Sam lead her to the indoor school.

But she was so tired from running around in the field that she couldn't keep up.

When Marion told them to canter,
Jenny could only do a slow trot.

After the lesson, Marion did not look happy.

'I don't like having my horses looking a mess,' she said. 'And I don't like them ignoring me in lessons.'

Marion frowned. 'Perhaps
Jenny is too naughty to take part
in lessons.'

'Fine,' Jenny thought. 'More
time to hang out with my friends.'

But then Marion added, 'That
rules her out of the Spring Gala too.'

The Spring Gala? Wait. Wasn't that the thing that was making everyone sing and smile and whistle?

Jenny wasn't so happy now.

Chapter Three

Marion clapped her hands. 'Mrs Andrews is here for her lesson. Is Jazz tacked up and ready?'

Jazz was the tallest, smartest horse on the yard. She walked past Jenny with her nose in the air.

Jenny watched Mrs Andrews greet Jazz with a handful of mints.

She watched as Mrs Andrews gave another packet to a boy who was with her. 'These are for the horses, remember, James, not for you.'

Mrs Andrews bent down to kiss him, then smoothed his hair down.

'Yes, Grandma,' James said, as
he reached up and ruffled his hair
back up again.

'Ha!' Jenny thought. 'He's
like me.'

Jenny looked closer. James wasn't like all the others. Most of them only had legs. James had some very cool wheels as well.

James looked across at Jenny and smiled. Then he reached down and pushed his shiny wheels across the yard towards her.

'He's the same height as me,'
Jenny thought. Most people
looked down at Jenny. James
looked her right in the eyes.

'Can I groom her?' James asked.
Sophie was trying to groom Jenny
as she yanked her head this way
and that.

'You'll be lucky,' replied Sophie.

James took the brush from Sophie. 'I don't like having my hair brushed either,' he said to Jenny.

Jenny stood absolutely still.
She let James brush her. When he
pulled too hard and she winced,
he stopped and stroked her before
giving her a mint and starting
again.

Sophie looked on in silence
as James got all the mud out of
Jenny's mane.

When he'd finished, he reached out to her and Jenny nuzzled into his arms. He was the perfect height for that too.

'Good girl,' he said, and gave
her another mint.

Chapter Four

The next day, Mrs Andrews was back at the stables. 'I'd like to book a lesson,' she said to Marion, 'for my grandson.'

Jenny's ears pricked up.

'He's never ridden before, so
we need a horse who is stable and
gentle.'

Jenny's ears stood on end.

'And he's only small, so we need a little pony.'

Jenny's ears nearly went through the roof.

'Me, me, me!' Jenny thought.

'Hmmm,' Marion said. 'Well, there is one pony we could try.'

Sophie led Jenny out of her stable. 'Come on, let's get you to the mounting block,' she said.

Jenny had other ideas. She
pulled and whinnied and tried
to drag Sophie in the opposite
direction.

'I'm so sorry, I don't think she
wants to be ridden,' Sophie said.

'Yes I do!' thought Jenny.

'Yes she does!' said James. He
wheeled himself over to Jenny's side.

'Let her lead the way', said James. Sophie did what James said.

Jenny walked to her favourite spot by the hay bales. 'Can't play today,' she said to Sooty and Hobnob. 'I've got work to do.'

She waited while James
wheeled himself up the ramp.

She stood perfectly still as
James moved out of his chair and
clambered onto Jenny's back,
with help from Mrs Andrews and
Sophie.

Once James was settled, Jenny let Sophie lead them into the indoor school.

When Marion said walk, James clicked his tongue and Jenny walked. When Marion said stop, James pulled on the reins, and Jenny slowed down and stopped.

'I've found the perfect pony for me to ride,' thought James.

'I've found the perfect person to ride me,' thought Jenny.

Chapter Five

It was the day of the Spring Gala and the yard was busy. Horses were being groomed, manes combed, tails plaited and tack cleaned.

James was wearing a smart blue jacket, and his wheels were so shiny they sparkled.

The loudspeaker crackled. 'Jenny and James to the ring, please.'

James gave Jenny one last
brush so she shone in the sun.
Then he wheeled across the yard
to their mounting spot. Jade
helped James climb aboard.

'Good luck Jenny,' said James.

'Good luck James,' thought Jenny.

And in they went.

Jenny and James stood in front of the judge.

James gave a little bow.

Then they walked in a circle to the left and a circle to the right.

When James gave Jenny their special signal – a gentle flick of the reins – Jenny moved into the most graceful trot.

At the end, everyone cheered.

And when Jade helped James back into his chair, the first thing he did was hand Jenny a mint.

'Good girl,' he said as he stroked her mane.

Soon it was the end of the day
and the results were announced.
James stroked Jenny's nose as
Marion announced the winners,
one by one. She came to the last
category.

'With the best teamwork between horse and rider, the winners of the Junior Show Class are … Jenny and James!'

'We won!' James yelled. He opened his arms for Jenny and she nuzzled into him. James smiled as Marion handed him two bright ribbons – one for him, one for Jenny.

'Teamwork, that's all it takes,' thought Jenny, as James pinned the ribbon on her bridal and kissed her nose.

'And maybe a handful of mints.'